Aziza's
·Secret Fairy·
Door
and the
Mermaid's Treasure

Other books by Lola Morayo

Aziza's Secret Fairy Door

*Aziza's Secret Fairy Door and the
Ice Cat Mystery*

*Aziza's Secret Fairy Door and the
Birthday Present Disaster*

Coming soon!

*Aziza's Secret Fairy Door
and the Magic Puppy*

Aziza's
· Secret Fairy ·
Door
and the
Mermaid's Treasure

Lola Morayo

Illustrated by Cory Reid

MACMILLAN CHILDREN'S BOOKS

With special thanks to Tọ́lá Okogwu

Published 2022 by Macmillan Children's Books
an imprint of Pan Macmillan
The Smithson, 6 Briset Street, London EC1M 5NR
EU representative: Macmillan Publishers Ireland Ltd, 1st Floor,
The Liffey Trust Centre, 117–126 Sheriff Street Upper
Dublin 1, D01 YC43
Associated companies throughout the world
www.panmacmillan.com

ISBN 978-1-5290-6399-8

Text copyright © Storymix Limited 2022
Illustrations copyright © Cory Reid 2022
Series created by Storymix Limited.
Edited by Jasmine Richards.

The right of Storymix Limited and Cory Reid to be identified as the
author and illustrator of this work has been asserted by them
in accordance with the Copyright, Designs and Patents Act 1988.

1 3 5 7 9 8 6 4 2

A CIP catalogue record for this book is available from the British Library.

Printed and bound by CPI Group (UK) Ltd, Croydon CR0 4YY

FSC
www.fsc.org
MIX
Paper | Supporting
responsible forestry
FSC® C116313

To all the aspiring writers out there.
Your words matter.

T. O.

For Michaela Olufunmilayo Ashaye.
Although far away, always close
to her daddy's heart.

J. R.

For all adventurers

C. R.

Chapter 1

The sound of heavy rain beating against the window echoed across the living room. Aziza stared glumly at the big fat droplets sliding down the fogged-up glass. *It's supposed to be summer*, she thought.

'Has anyone seen the tent?' bellowed Dad from the hallway. 'I need to get it into the car first, so we can see how much space we have left for the rest of the camping stuff.'

Aziza poked her head into the corridor. She could only see half of her dad. The other half was deep inside a cupboard. He

was surrounded by boxes of the Jamal Justice graphic novels that Aziza's mum and dad wrote. Jamal Justice was a really popular character, and the books took up loads of space in the flat.

'Nope, no tent!' hollered Otis, as he leapt over the boxes of books and then dodged

past the piles of camping gear to finally get into the living room. He flopped down on the sofa. 'I did find my rucksack, though, and look.' He held up a greyish-looking square and waved it at Aziza. 'I even found a piece of chocolate from last year's trip.'

Otis popped the prize into his mouth.

'Eww,' Aziza squealed at her brother.

'Otis, what have I told you about eating unidentifiable objects?' Mum said with a frown as she entered from the kitchen.

'Sorry, Mum,' Otis said with a chocolatey

grin. 'I need to keep my energy up if we're going camping.'

'Camping,' Mum muttered. 'When I married your father, he promised hearts and flowers. He didn't say anything about soggy tents.'

'Come on, honey,' Dad said, striding into the room. A long, red bag was cradled in his arms. 'I've found the tent now. It's all good.'

Mum raised an eyebrow. 'Good? Have you seen the weather?'

'I'm sure it will get better,' Aziza piped up.

Mum sighed and looked longingly at the

glossy holiday magazine on the side table. She picked it up and waved it in the air.

'Just look at this: sun, sea and sand,' she said. 'It would have been simply superb.'

Dad grabbed the magazine, a wide grin splitting his face. 'Superb kindling for a fire, you mean.'

'We'll need a fire!' Mum replied with a snort. 'It's freezing out there.'

Dad laughed and Aziza watched as Mum playfully tried to retrieve the magazine. Aziza had been really looking forward to the trip. They had tried camping for the first time last year and it had been great. But it had also been dry. *If we are going to be stuck in that tiny tent together for a whole week, I'd better take some books with me.*

'I'm going to finish packing,' Aziza said, leaving her parents and Otis behind and heading to her room.

Resting on her sparkly Fairy Power duvet was Aziza's half-filled rucksack. Aziza looked round her room to find the latest Fairy Power book. She froze when she spotted a thin trail of golden sand and tiny seashells dusting her windowsill and leading past Lil, her pot plant, and right up to the . . . secret fairy door.

Small fragments of smooth sea glass were studded into the door, making it sparkle like a coloured mosaic. The door stood slightly ajar as if it were inviting Aziza to go through.

She shivered with excitement. *It's time to go back to the magical kingdom of Shimmerton!* Aziza hesitated for a moment and glanced back at her rucksack. *But what about the holiday?* Then she remembered. Time moved faster in Shimmerton. *I'll be back before Dad has even put that tent in the car!*

Aziza touched the sparkly doorknob and immediately she felt herself start to shrink. This time she didn't hesitate, and she ran straight through the fairy door. Bright sunshine greeted her on the other side and Aziza blinked in wonder at the sandy beach stretching out in front of her, leading towards a deep-blue sea.

The sun blazed down from a cloudless pink sky, warming her bare shoulders. Aziza looked down to find her jeans and T-shirt were gone, replaced by a cute playsuit that matched the

colours of her butterfly wings. *Wow*. Aziza did a small spin. She could feel the wings fluttering behind her. *I'm definitely not home any more.* The fairy door was shut tight again. Its edges blended invisibly into the trunk of a large palm tree. If you didn't know it was there, you wouldn't even notice it.

Just then a beach ball bounced past Aziza and a small Almiraj sprinted after it. His long bunny ears trailed in the wind behind him. In fact, the beach was packed full of Shimmerton residents having fun.

Music filled the air, and the leaves of the palm trees seemed to sway in time to the beat. At the edge of the beach was a huge barbecue. The pharmacist Mr Phoenix stood next to it. Flames burst from his bright-red feathers keeping the grill hot, while two ogres chatted as they waited in line to be served their halloumi kebabs.

In the water was Neith the weaver. She was whizzing along on a giant inflatable potato. Golden sparkles seemed to cover her and Aziza realized that the inflatable must be powered by some kind of magic.

It feels like carnival weekend, Aziza thought, looking at everybody's smiling faces, as they ate and danced and laughed with each other.

But where are Tiko and Peri? Aziza searched through the crowd, trying to find her friends.

'You're having a laugh!' an outraged voice suddenly protested. 'Our castle is not a hazard.'

Aziza stood on tiptoe and spotted Kendra, Noon and Felly standing by a very tall sandcastle. It had turrets and *even* balconies.

Kendra was busy waving a sand-covered shovel in the air as she spoke. 'It's totally epic,' Noon agreed, dodging flying sand. 'And we totally didn't move anyone's chair, picnic blanket or swimming trunks to make space,' Felly added.

Kendra rolled her eyes, and Noon elbowed Felly sharply.

'What?' Felly grumbled, rubbing her side.

Ugh, of course the Gigglers are here and making a drama as usual, Aziza thought.

'Young ladies, sandcastles must adhere to strict size limits.' Officer Alf appeared from the other side of the sandcastle. He had his elf and safety clipboard in one hand and a tape measure in the other. 'You cannot just go about moving sand around.'

'Why not?' Noon asked.

Officer Alf sighed. 'Because—'

'You're just jealous,' Kendra interrupted with a roll of her eyes. 'Because we're the queens of the beach.'

The Elf and Safety Officer's mouth dropped open in shock and the three fairies giggled. He then jabbed at some notes on his clipboard and started to tell them that all this digging was very disruptive and . . .

Aziza gasped as she spotted a small bearlike creature just a few metres away by the sea shore. It was her friend Tiko! *And look, there's Peri too*, Aziza thought as she started to run towards the fairy princess with swan-like wings.

As Aziza got closer, she realized that Peri and Tiko were trying to skim stones across the water and they weren't alone. Next to them, sitting on a rock that was being lapped by the waves, was a pretty girl with the longest locs Aziza had ever seen. In her hand was a stone and, as she threw it, it danced perfectly across the waves until it disappeared out of sight.

I wonder who she . . . but the thought was

left unfinished as she realized something

amazing. 'Glittersticks!' Aziza breathed.

The new girl was a mermaid. An actual

mermaid!

Chapter 2

'Aziza!' Peri squealed, running over to hug her. 'I'm so glad you're here.'

'When did you arrive?' Tiko gave her a hug also.

'Not long ago.' Aziza nodded shyly at the

mermaid, unable to take her eyes off her tail.

It glittered so brightly in the water, sparkling

with shades of emerald and sapphire.

'Hi Aziza,' the mermaid said with a grin.

'I'm Sirena.'

'Sirena's mum is best friends with my mum so we've known each other for ages,' Peri added. 'But we only get to see her when we come to the ocean.'

'It's totally annoying not to see each other more often,' Sirena tucked one of her long locs behind her ear, 'but mermaids belong in the water. That's just the way it is.'

Oh, that must be why I didn't meet her at Peri's birthday party, Aziza realized.

Tiko smiled sympathetically at Sirena. 'Your home is awesome, though, and your mum is amazing, too. I mean, she's the mother of the ocean after all. How cool must it be looking after all of the sea creatures, and solving all their problems.'

'I know. Mum is pretty cool! I'm proud of all her hard work.' Sirena held out a small, smooth stone. 'Aziza, would you like to have a go?'

Aziza felt her cheeks getting warm with embarrassment. 'I don't know how to skip stones.'

Sirena grinned. 'It's easy. Watch, I'll show you.' With a flick of her wrist, Sirena sent the pebble flying across the water. It skipped so many times, Aziza lost count.

Aziza stared doubtfully after it. *That doesn't look easy.*

'Come on,' Peri cried with an encouraging smile.

'Yeah, you can do it,' Tiko added.

Aziza picked up a flat stone. 'OK, I'll give it a go!' She flung the pebble hard. It sailed through the air, hit the water . . . and then sank.

'Try again,' Peri encouraged with a gentle smile, handing Aziza another stone.

Aziza took a deep breath, then threw the

24

stone again with all her might. Again, it sank without even a single bounce. Aziza's shoulders sagged. *Why can't I get it right?*

'That's OK, you'll get it next time,' Sirena said reassuringly. 'I remember when I first tried. My pebble sank straight down

and almost hit a baby seahorse on the head. That's how I met Water Dancer. She's my pet but is visiting her cousins right now.'

Aziza tried not to gape. 'You have a pet seahorse? That's so cool.'

'Yeah, I guess it is.' Sirena picked up another stone and expertly skipped it across the waves again. 'We're always going on adventures and hunting for treasure. This one time, we were searching a shipwreck when we were almost trapped by a shark. Luckily it had a bad cold and we managed to escape because it was sneezing so much. It was wild!'

Aziza stared at Sirena. *Treasure-hunting? Escaping sharks? Sirena is out of this world.*

'Then there was the time we discovered a whole abandoned city underwater,' Sirena continued. 'All the buildings were made of gold and it was guarded by a giant sea monster . . .'

Sirena's voice trailed off as a mighty rumble shook the sand and the ground began to tremble.

'Arrgh!!!' Aziza's arms windmilled as she tried to stay upright. 'What's going on?'

'Oh, not again,' Peri huffed and zoomed up into the air.

Meanwhile, Tiko had curled up into a furry ball that rolled about as the ground trembled beneath him.

'This is fun,' Sirena giggled, doing her best to stay balanced on the rock she was sitting on.

Aziza frowned. 'Since when is an earthquake fun?' She took a step forwards but another tremor shook the ground, sending her tumbling into the warm sand.

Peri zoomed down and held out a hand to pull her up. 'It's not an earthquake. This

happens sometimes on Shimmerton Beach
when a shell-walker sneezes.'

'When a what sneezes?' Aziza asked.

'Shell-walkers are creatures that live really
deep underground near the sea and sleep all

day.' Tiko replied in a muffled voice. He was still in a ball.

'You don't need to be scared, Aziza,' Sirena said.

'I wasn't scared.' Aziza briskly brushed the sand off her playsuit. Something about Sirena's words was really annoying. 'I just didn't know what was going on. I mean, I've never even seen a shell-walker.'

'Well, no one has,' Sirena replied with a flick of her locs.

Tiko unfurled as the tremors finally stopped. 'They're really deep sleepers and if they ever wake up, it's always at night.'

'I see,' Aziza said. She looked around the beach. Everyone had gone back to laughing and chatting. No one seemed bothered about the tremors at all. Aziza bit her lip. 'It's just, where I come from, tremors are a BAD thing!'

'How about a game of splash ball?' Peri suggested. 'That will make you forget all about the tremors. I'll go and borrow a ball.'

Sirena clapped her hands. 'Ooh, I love splash ball. Just let me collect Water Dancer first. She loves it too.'

The mermaid slipped under the water, her

glittering tail flashing behind her.

Peri went to hunt down a ball, leaving just Tiko and Aziza at the water's edge.

Tiko gently nudged Aziza. 'Are you OK?'

'I'm good, I guess I was just freaked out about those tremors,' Aziza replied.

'I know what will cheer you up. I'm going to grab some ice lollies.' Tiko pointed to an ice cream van that was nearby. 'Stay here and save our spot.'

Aziza nodded, still feeling a bit silly about how worried she'd been.

'Hey! Where are my tongs?' called a

frazzled voice. It
was Mr Phoenix. His
flaming feathers bristled
with annoyance.
'They've gone
missing.'

'So has my
bucket and spade,'
cried a grumpy-
looking gnome.

'And MY beach towel,' roared a very wet

cyclops. Water dripped down his eye.

'Why are you sitting in my deck chair?'

a pixie yelled at his friend.

'This is my deck chair, I'll have you know,' the other pixie replied.

'Where's mine gone, then?'

'I don't know,' the friend screeched back. 'It's not like I can hide a whole chair behind my back.'

Oh dear, it must be the heat making everyone grumpy, thought Aziza. *Otis gets grouchy too when he gets too hot.*

Just then, Tiko

returned with a pair of brightly coloured ice lollies in each hand.

'Which flavour do you want?' He asked cheerfully. 'Whisperberry dreams, or youngerflower giggles?'

Before Aziza could reply, the ice lollies shot out of Tiko's grasp. They spun through the air so fast that Aziza quickly lost sight of them.

Tiko stared at Aziza. 'What just happened?'

Aziza shook her head. 'I don't know, I

thought it must be another Shimmerton thing!'

At that moment, Peri appeared. She had a big red beach ball tucked under her arm. 'You won't believe what I just saw. Flying ice lollies, I kid you not.'

Peri had barely finished speaking when the beach ball was ripped from under her arm and went zooming through the air.

'Glittersticks,' Aziza breathed.

'Oi,' Peri called, chasing after it. 'Come back here.'

Aziza and Tiko followed Peri.

'Duck,' Tiko suddenly cried as a picnic basket whooshed over his head.

Aziza only *just* managed to get out of the way as food rained down from the flying basket. Aziza gasped as she spotted a beach chair tumbling through the air and a frazzled-looking pixie sprinting after it. The strangest part of all was that the items all seemed to be heading in the same direction . . . towards the Gigglers!

Chapter 3

'I should have known you lot would have something to do with . . . well, whatever this is.' Peri said as they reached the Gigglers.

Aziza shook her head as she looked at all the stuff that was piled up next to the giant sandcastle. 'How did you even make all this stuff come to you?' she asked.

'And why?' Tiko added.

'What are you going on about?' squeaked Noon. 'We haven't done anything.'

Kendra put her hands on her hips. 'Yeah, we've been busy building our epic castle. That's it.'

Felly nodded. 'All the flying stuff has absolutely nothing to do with us or the giant hole that we dug to make our sandcastle.'

Kendra groaned. 'Felly! You really are rubbish at keeping a secret.'

'Whoops,' Felly said. 'Well at least I haven't told them that we've woken something u—'

The rest of Felly's sentence was cut off by Kendra's hand clamping over her mouth.

'All right,' Peri demanded. 'Fess up.'

The Gigglers stared back mutinously until at last, Kendra sighed. 'Fine. We might have been making too much noise with all our digging.'

'Maybe we dug too deep,' Noon added. 'But there was some kind of creature down there.'

'Not that we got a proper look before all

this stuff came flying at us,' Kendra explained.

Felly bounced on the spot. 'I got a proper look. It looked a bit like a tiny dragon, but it was covered in grey shells. Then it disappeared when all this stuff turned up.' She pointed at the pile.

Kendra beat her wings and rose up into the air. 'Anyway, you're here now and you love sorting stuff out so we're going to leave you to it. We'd hate to get in the way.'

Felly and Noon took flight also. 'See ya, wouldn't wanna be ya!' Kendra yelled as the three fairies flew off.

'That's so typical of them,' Peri huffed, glaring after the Gigglers. 'They cause the problem and then leave it to us to sort out.'

Aziza sighed. 'Well, at least it is not a big problem. Felly said it was a tiny dragon. Do you think it is under this pile of stuff?'

'Maybe.' Tiko sounded puzzled. 'But I've never heard of a shell-covered dragon before.'

Suddenly there was a sneezing sound and the ground shuddered for a moment. A memory of something Tiko and Sirena had said tickled the back of Aziza's mind. 'Could it be a . . . a shell-walker?' she asked.

Peri gasped. 'No way . . . it couldn't . . . could it?' Her voice faltered.

Tiko gulped. 'But they *never ever* come out in the day. My mum says they are super dangerous.'

'But Felly said the creature was tiny,' Peri said. 'Shell-walkers are like . . . huge.' Aziza was glad to hear this. She kind of loved the idea of meeting a baby dragon. Just then, a small tail flicked out of the pile of stuff. Immediately, a pink snorkel flew towards the heap and the whole pile seemed to move as things shifted about to make room for the snorkel.

Tiko's face creased into a grimace. 'Don't you see? The shell-walker is attracting all this stuff – that's what they do. That's how it got its shells in the first place. But as it grows in size, its grabbing force will get stronger, and it'll start attracting even bigger things!'

'If it doesn't go back to sleep soon, it's going to become huge,' Peri added. 'And then what if it leaves the beach? Shimmerton will be in real trouble.'

'It will grab all the houses in town,' Aziza gasped in understanding.

Tiko's little nose began to twitch. 'The

trees in the Wailing Woods.'

'The rocks on the Ice Mountain,' they all said at once.

'We've got to stop it,' Aziza cried. We need to—'

'Ask Sirena,' Peri finished triumphantly. 'Think about all those amazing adventures she's been on.' Peri continued. 'She's always solving problems. I bet she'll know what to do.'

Tiko nodded eagerly. 'That's a great idea. Let's go before the shell-walker decides to leave this hole.'

'All right,' said Aziza.

Tiko and Peri raced back to the shoreline. Aziza followed but kept looking over her shoulder to make sure the shell-walker was still in the same place and under the ground.

We really don't have much time, Aziza thought.

'Hey, you're back,' Sirena said from her rock.

'Sorry we took so long.' Peri quickly filled her in on the situation with the shell-walker.

'We need to find a way to get it back to sleep, or it will destroy Shimmerton,' Aziza said.

'And we thought you might have a plan,' Tiko finished.

Aziza thought she saw a flash of uncertainty on the mermaid's face but realized she must be wrong. Sirena was so confident, how could she ever be uncertain about anything?

Bobbing in the water beside
her was a beautiful pink
seahorse, whose bright
eyes sparkled above her
long snout.

Sirena tapped her chin
for a moment, then her face lit
up. 'I know exactly what we need to do. My
mum told me about this legend once . . . that
there's a magical conch shell somewhere that
plays a special song that will help you solve
any problem.'

'Magic shell that plays a song?' Peri

repeated. 'That sounds perfect!'

'We just need to go into the ocean and find it,' Sirena finished with a confident smile.

'If anyone can find it, it's you!' Tiko declared. 'You're the best treasure-hunter in all of Shimmerton. Remember the time you and Water Dancer discovered that cursed treasure in the cave of doom? I love it when you tell us about that adventure.'

Sirena's confident smile slipped for a second. 'Erm . . . yeah.'

Peri nodded. 'Or that time you defeated the ship full of pirates? Looking for the magic conch shell will be easy-peasy compared to that.'

'Sure, but I'd still love your help finding it,' Sirena said. 'We can all go on an ocean adventure together.'

'Yay! We love going underwater,' Tiko and Peri whooped with delight.

Aziza stared at her feet. She worked really hard at her swimming and she loved it, but somehow she didn't think she'd be able to keep up with a mermaid. *And how am I supposed to breathe underwater?* Tiko could shape-shift but could fairies breathe underwater?

'Aziza, don't look so worried,' Sirena said. 'I'll help you swim underwater.'

Sirena's smile was friendly but somehow that made Aziza feel even worse. Why was this mermaid so great at everything? 'I wasn't worried,' she muttered.

'Oh, OK,' Sirena said breezily. 'I just thought I'd use my magic to turn you guys into mermaids.'

'You have magic as well?' Aziza asked.

'Yeah, it was a birthday gift from my mum a while back,' Sirena said.

Peri squealed. 'It's so much fun, you get a

tail and everything.' Her face creased into a frown as a crunching sound filled the air.

Aziza spun round to see that the shell-walker was on the move. It was the strangest sight. A huge pile of stuff waddled across the beach and towards the promenade. Alf, the Elf and Safety Officer, was standing a few metres away waving a red beach towel at the shell-walker as if trying to get its attention. Mr Bracken was on all fours, horn down. Pawing at the ground.

'What are they doing?' Aziza asked.

Peri frowned. 'I think they're trying to get

the shell-walker back into the hole. Looks like Mr Bracken is going to charge.'

'That's not going to work,' Sirena cried. 'Come on, follow me!' She slipped into the water, her seahorse bobbing next to her, then traced a symbol on the surface that began to glow. 'Don't worry, it's just my magic.'

Peri didn't need a second invitation. With a loud squeal, she jumped into the shimmering water, disappearing beneath the waves. Then up Peri sprang, her feathery wings spread wide. Her new silver tail gleamed under the sun before she landed again with a splash. Droplets of water hit Aziza and Tiko, who were still standing on the shore.

'Careful,' Tiko grumbled.

Wow, Aziza thought. She loved swimming, and a part of her couldn't wait to transform into a mermaid, too. But another part of her was nervous. *What if I can't swim well with a tail? And will I really be able to swim underwater? How do I even breathe?*

'Let's go,' Sirena said, but Tiko shook his head.

'No offence, but I didn't love being a merperson last time,' he said. 'It's not easy to swim with that tail if you're not used to it.'

He took a deep breath then leapt into the air, his eyes shut and his face scrunched in concentration.

He's shape-shifting, Aziza realized. *I wonder*

if he'll turn into a seahorse like Water Dancer, or

maybe a dolphin.

With a flash of sparkles, Tiko's furry body

disappeared, replaced instead by a round

scaly one, with sharp teeth, a dorsal fin and

a strange thing between his eyes that glowed.

He dropped into the water.

'An anglerfish?

Sirena said.

'When you

could have

been a

merperson?'

'Oh dear,' Peri said. 'Did you mean to do that?'

'Yes, I meant to,' Tiko huffed. 'Anglerfish are the coolest.' Tiko shook his head and the lure between his eyes glowed brighter. 'See? I even have my own light.'

'That *is* pretty magical,' Aziza replied, impressed. 'But I'd much rather be a mermaid!' She ran towards the water.

Chapter 4

A strange tingling began in Aziza's toes and with each step she took, it grew stronger, stretching up her legs. Then suddenly, she was no longer kicking, but floating in the water. Aziza looked down to find a beautiful golden tail where her legs used to be.

Glittersticks! I'm an actual mermaid. The scales

on her tail sparkled beneath the crystal-clear

water. She quickly looked over her shoulder.

Cool, I've still got my wings, too!

'Try diving under the water,' Peri suggested with a grin.

Aziza took a deep breath and plunged into the water, her tail flapping about behind her. Almost immediately, Aziza bobbed back up

to the surface. *That's not right.* She tried again but couldn't get her tail to work properly.

Then she felt someone take her hand. It was Sirena, and beside her was Water Dancer.

'Here, let me help,' Sirena said gently.

Aziza hesitated for a moment, then nodded. The mermaid plunged into the water, taking Aziza with her. Aziza took a big gulp of air before the water closed around her. She was so busy trying not to panic that it took a moment for her to realize she was now under the water.

'You don't need to hold your breath, you

know,' Sirena's grin was wide. 'You can breathe and talk under water just like me.'

I can do this, Aziza thought to herself. Then she braced herself and took a deep breath. Cool air magically filled her lungs and Aziza finally relaxed. *I'm doing it. I can breathe.*

'Watch me,' Sirena suggested, letting go of Aziza's hand. 'If you wiggle your tail like this, you can stay afloat and move forwards without even using your arms.'

Aziza copied Sirena's rhythmic movements and her body shot forwards, moving smoothly through the water. '*Wow*, that's so much fun,' Aziza said.

Sirena grinned. 'I'm glad you like it down here.'

Aziza grinned back.

Peri and Tiko joined them.

'So, Sirena, where do we go now?'

Aziza saw a flash of panic on Sirena's face. 'Erm . . . the thing is, I'm not sure.'

'Not sure?' Tiko squeaked.

'I thought you knew where to find the conch shell!' Peri exclaimed.

'Oh no, I didn't mean I wasn't sure about that,' Sirena said quickly, with a flick of her glittery tail. 'You interrupted me. I meant . . . I'm not sure you'll be able to keep up with me – I'm a treasure-hunter extraordinaire, after all!'

The mermaid laughed, but to Aziza's ears it seemed as if she was trying a bit too hard to sound cheerful. 'So, you're sure that—'

'When Mum told me the legend of the conch she said it could be found "near the jewel that can be found in the deep". That's got to mean the shipwreck at the very bottom of the ocean, right? It has lots of treasures and jewels.'

'But . . .' Aziza stopped as she felt a tap on her shoulder.

It was Tiko's little orange fin. 'Sirena's great at coming up with ideas,' he said, the lamp hanging from his forehead bouncing about. 'So you don't need to worry. I promise.'

Aziza sighed and shrugged. 'OK, let's get to that ship.'

They zoomed through the turquoise water, Sirena swimming ahead. The deeper they went, the cooler the water got, although Aziza didn't feel cold inside. *Is this mermaid magic?* she wondered.

A shoal of bright-yellow
fish streamed by, and Sirena
waved.

'Hi, Sirena!' the
fish all seemed to
say as one, in light,
squeaky voices. 'Have a nice day!'

Aziza turned to watch
the fish swim away. 'How
can I can understand

what they're saying?' she asked. Tiny bubbles
popped from her mouth as she spoke.

Sirena spun around and winked. 'It's part of the mermaid magic. You can understand all sea creatures. Amazing, right?'

Aziza nodded. It *was* amazing. She wanted to ask the sea creatures all sorts of questions, but she knew there wasn't time for that. Who knew what was happening with the shell-walker up on shore? She really hoped Officer Alf and Mr Bracken had got the shell-walker back into its hole!

They kept on swimming, Aziza wriggling her tail just like Sirena had shown her. The water flowed over her body and wings like the softest fabric. *I'm a MERMAID*, she told

herself. *A fairy mermaid!*

Up ahead, Sirena suddenly stopped and

Aziza saw that she was talking to a creature.

A pink dolphin!

As she neared her friends, she heard Sirena explaining what had happened on shore.

The dolphin shook its fins, looking horrified. 'That does not sound good. I should go to Shimmerton and help.'

'But . . . how will you survive out of the ocean?' Aziza asked, confused. If Sirena wasn't supposed to leave the water, surely this dolphin couldn't either.

'Oh, my friend Cante here is an Encantado!' Sirena drawled. 'He can totally shape-shift into human form, no problem.'

Cante nodded. 'I can indeed. We're very

clever, you know!' He shot off through the water, waving his tail as if in goodbye.

Aziza breathed out a stream of bubbles in a sigh of relief. She was still worried about the shell-walker leaving the beach and heading for the centre of Shimmerton. But hopefully now, thanks to Cante, they would have a bit more time to find the magical conch shell.

'Let's go!' said Peri, diving down, folding back her feathery wings as she whizzed through the water. The others followed, and Sirena quickly took the lead again to show them the way.

Soon, Aziza's tail was starting to feel sore from all the swimming. *The shipwreck has to be close n—!* The thought was chased away as she spotted something incredible up ahead.

Is that a CORAL REEF? She'd seen coral reefs on the TV documentaries her mum liked to watch, but this was a whole other level of beautiful. It was like a piece of art

in the ocean, with its rainbow colours –
pink, purple, turquoise, yellow, orange, red.
She couldn't stop staring at it, noticing that
every part of the reef was different –

some coral waved gently in the water, some seemed to pulse, other parts fluttered as fish brushed against the fronds. The coral seemed to shimmer and glow in the ocean, as if it was powered by electricity, lighting it up. Aziza was sure the water was warmer here, too – like the perfect bubble bath. She flicked her tail hard to shoot forward faster than before, and was soon nose-to-nose with a shoal of black-and-white-striped fish.

They flittered around her, tickling her skin and golden tail.

'They're three-stripe damsel fish,' Sirena called out behind her.

'They look like humbugs.' Aziza grinned. Humbugs were her gran's favourite sweets. Aziza swam further forward, towards a patch of shimmering peachy-coloured coral, shaped like little fans. It looked so soft, and the sparkly fans waved at her, calling her closer.

'Nooo!' shouted Sirena, and Aziza felt a tug on her tail. The mermaid was determinedly pulling Aziza away from the coral reef. 'You can't touch it!' Sirena explained. 'You shouldn't touch coral anyway, but especially not this. It's magical. Don't you see the shimmering sparkles around it?'

Aziza flicked her head back around to look, *oh yeah, the coral is definitely covered in sparkle*s, she thought.

'The coral has special healing powers,' Sirena continued. 'You shouldn't take any of that healing magic when you don't need it. It's for injured creatures, who come here when they need help.'

Glittersticks. Aziza suddenly felt terrible. She needed to be more careful around here. She didn't know anything about Shimmerton's magical ocean. 'I'm so sorry. But I didn't touch it, I promise!'

Sirena nodded and let go of Aziza's tail, then started to lead them forwards once more.

For the first time in the water, Aziza felt cold inside, frustrated with herself for being so careless.

'Don't be upset,' Peri said, swimming to her side. 'You didn't mean any harm.' She lowered her voice and added, 'I did the same thing the first time I swam with Sirena. The coral looks so beautiful you can't help but want to touch it!'

Aziza's insides relaxed and she smiled at her friend. 'Thank you.'

Peri grabbed her hand and zoomed forward. Aziza squealed with delight as she flew through the ocean with her friend, faster than ever before.

Moments later, Aziza saw something in the distance. It was just as stunning as the coral, but in a different way. A beautiful old ship, lying on its side on the seabed. Its golden timber gleamed in the sunlight that trickled into the ocean from above. It was huge – at least the length of three double-decker buses. The sides were dotted with perfectly circular portholes and the ship had a carved creature at the bow – it looked like an octopus.

Aziza swam faster

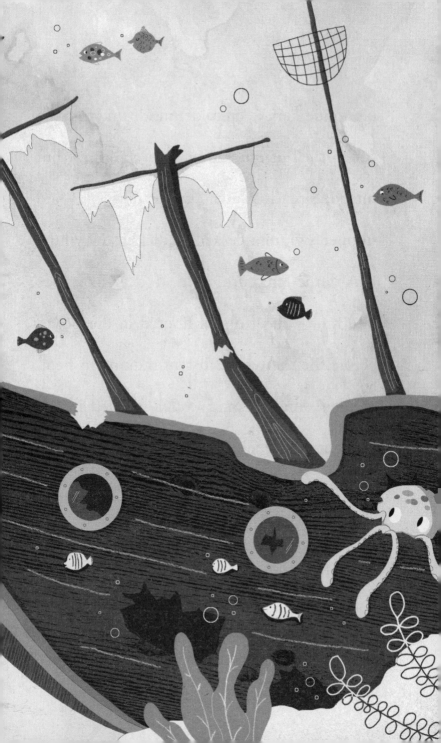

alongside Peri, keen to get inside and find the conch shell as quickly as they could . . . but ahead, Sirena, Water Dancer and Tiko had stopped swimming. Aziza quickly saw why.

A large creature with a deer-like face and the body of a seal floated in the ocean before the shipwreck. It was shaking its head at them, and its long antlers flashed in the sunlight that reached below the surface of the water.

Sirena, Water Dancer and Tiko swam away from the creature. They looked sad.

'Um, what is that?' Aziza asked in a

whisper. 'What was it saying?'

Sirena looked at Aziza, her eyes wide. 'That's a Makara and she won't allow us to go any further. She's saying we can't go onto the ship!'

Chapter 5

Aziza realized she must have looked as confused as she felt because Sirena quickly carried on explaining: 'You see, Makaras are creatures that protect gateways and thresholds.'

'It's kind of their thing,' Tiko added.

Peri frowned. 'Can't we ask her really nicely to let us past? Or tell her it's an emergency! We need to get the conch shell!'

Sirena shook her head, making her long locs swirl around her in the turquoise water. 'It's way more complicated than that,' she said. 'You always have to solve a riddle to get past a Makara. And the riddle she told me was really hard. We're never going to solve it.'

Aziza bit her lip. She didn't feel like they should give up before they'd even had a

proper go at it. 'Who says we can't solve it?'
Aziza said. 'Perhaps we just need to work
together!'

'But what if we get it wrong?' Tiko asked.

'Then we are no worse off,' Peri said. 'I agree with Aziza. Trying is the important bit!' Peri swam a little nearer to the Makara, her feathered wings tucked behind her.

Aziza breathed in deeply, felt cool air filling her lungs, and then flicked her tail to catch up with Peri. Looking over her shoulder, she saw Tiko and Sirena reluctantly following behind them.

Now that Aziza was closer, she could hear some of the words that the Makara was whispering. She closed her eyes to focus on what was being said and tried to tune out all

the other gurgling, swooshing, bubbling sounds of the ocean.

'*The name of this ship isn't one to forget.*

The answer allows you to enter the wreck.

It's soft yet spiky, and means true love.

A word with two meanings — you'll find it above.'

Aziza opened her eyes again. 'So, we have to guess the name of the ship!' she said.

They were all quiet for a moment, even Peri.

Then Tiko shouted, 'Unicorn!'

The others all looked at him, confused.

Unicorn? wondered Aziza.

Tiko flapped his little green fins. 'You know, because it's soft but also has a spiky horn, and because everyone truly loves it!'

'I'm not sure that's quite right,' Peri said. 'Does the word "unicorn" have two meanings?'

Tiko turned to face the Makara, bobbing in the water hopefully. But the creature

89

shook her deer-like head.

Aziza thought it through. What was soft and spiky? What kind of things meant true love? Perhaps a heart? Aziza suddenly remembered something her mum had said earlier that morning, about preferring flowers to soggy tents. *Could flowers mean love?*

Aziza tried to think of as many flowers as she could . . . daffodils . . . sunflowers . . . roses . . . Roses. Their petals were soft and their thorns spiky. Aziza gasped as she repeated the last line to herself: '*A word with two meanings – you'll find it above.*' Maybe the riddle wasn't just talking about any kind of flower, but a flower that also meant something else. A word with two meanings . . . with a name that meant 'above'. A name like Rose.

Aziza hesitated for a moment while the others kept guessing. She didn't want to look silly and get it wrong. But Tiko nudged her with his dangling lamp. 'You've got that look on your face. You've thought of something, haven't you?'

'I just . . . could it be . . . ? *Rose?*' Aziza asked. 'Because "rose" is a flower, but it

could also mean "rise", like "I rose from the sea", you know?'

'Genius!' said Sirena, beaming. They turned to the Makara, who'd stopped shaking her head and was now nodding instead. She stood to one side to let them past.

'You did it!' Peri said, flinging an arm around Aziza.

Flicking their tails, they swam past the Makara. She whispered again as they neared the ship: 'Congratulations, you passed the test. Now you may enter – good luck on your quest!'

I wonder how she knows we're on a quest, thought Aziza. *It must be more ocean magic!*

Closer up, *The Rose* looked even bigger than before. They swam towards the nearest porthole and Aziza saw it was edged with carved roses – well, that was a hint she had missed! She looked up at the rest of the ship. It made her neck ache to peer so high at the towering masts.

'Follow me!' Sirena said, ducking through the porthole. 'We'll soon find the conch shell – I'm an expert at treasure-hunting!'

Aziza followed Sirena and gasped as she

slipped inside the ship. It was much darker in here. '*Glittersticks!*' she said. 'I'm really glad we have you, Tiko!' The lamp on his head looked much brighter now in the darkness, and helped to light up the inside of the ship.

'See – being an anglerfish is awesome!' Tiko's lamp seemed to glow even stronger.

Peri nodded. 'You're right, Tiko!'

'OK! We need to stick together so no one gets lost,' Sirena said, beckoning the others closer.

Everyone agreed that was best. No one

wanted to get lost in a shipwreck, however beautiful it was.

They searched the deck for the conch shell, gently moving plants to check it wasn't hidden among the wildlife. They found

sparkling gems, golden coins and some bright sea crystals – but the conch shell was nowhere to be found.

Once they'd reached the end of the top deck, they went to explore the lower deck. Here there were fewer plants and treasures, but more sea creatures – purple crabs, blue-grey octopuses and even a couple of lobsters.

Aziza shuddered, spotting their large claws, but Sirena just smiled. 'They're harmless,' she drawled, turning to the lobsters. 'You won't hurt us, will you?'

When they clacked their claws together, it sounded like words. 'You mind your business and we'll mind ours.'

Aziza carried on looking. She'd been searching so long that her eyes were starting to ache. The conch shell wasn't down here either. What were they going to do?

'Where is it, Sirena?' Peri said, slumping to sit on the wooden beams of the floor.

Tiko bobbed by Peri's head. 'Sirena! You told us it would be here and it definitely isn't!'

Sirena bit her lip. 'Maybe I'm not so great at finding treasures.'

Aziza darted towards Sirena and patted her arm. 'Don't you remember? The first time you let us know about this shell you told us it was a legend. Well, sometimes legends can be wrong. Legends are just another word for story, after all . . . and stories are misremembered all the time!'

Sirena nodded miserably.

'OK, so what did the story say again?' Aziza asked gently. 'That the conch shell is on a shipwreck? Near the buried jewel?'

Now Sirena sank to the floor, hanging her head. Her locs were so long they touched the wooden floor in front of her. 'I just guessed that the conch would be on this shipwreck,' she mumbled. 'Mum didn't say anything about a shipwreck . . . just that the conch was where the buried jewel was.' Sirena rubbed at her eyes. 'I . . . I should have told you that I didn't know for sure. And . . . I didn't really go treasure-hunting in all those places I told you about. I just wanted to impress you. And now I've wasted time and the shell-walker could be destroying Shimmerton as we speak!'

Sirena rubbed at her eyes even more fiercely.

'Oh, don't cry!' Peri rushed to her friend and held her hand. 'It's not your fault – you were just trying to help.'

Sirena lifted her head up and wiped a tear from her cheek. 'But I shouldn't have exaggerated the way I did. And now I'm out of ideas. It's all my fault!'

Tiko's little light flashed, bathing Sirena's face in a soft glow. 'This isn't about blaming each other. We just have to work as a team! Isn't that what you said earlier, Aziza?'

Aziza nodded. 'I couldn't have said it better

myself Tiko and—' She gasped as something about the 'buried jewel' popped into her head. 'Hey, maybe this whole thing is just another kind of riddle!' she said. 'Could buried just mean somewhere "deep"? Maybe the conch shell is in a really deep part of the ocean? Somewhere near a different kind of jewel?'

Sirena tapped her chin and gave Aziza a grin. 'That's it. Aziza, you're right. The deepest place in the whole ocean is called the Opal Trench. And an opal is a jewel.' She frowned. 'There's just one problem, it's very, very far away . . .'

Chapter 6

They had been swimming for a long time now. Aziza wondered what might be happening above the water. What was the shell-walker doing right now? Had it got any bigger? Had it left the beach? *It will be fine,*

Aziza told herself as the group swam through the darkening water. *Cante, the pink dolphin, will be there helping* and *we'll bring back the conch shell and everything will be totally fine!*

Sirena began singing a song as they swam, and Aziza moved closer so she could hear the words. Sirena had a beautiful voice – rich and warm. It instantly made Aziza feel less worried.

'I can teach you the words, if you'd like,' Sirena offered. 'It's a song that creatures in the ocean sing about my mother. It is better in a group anyway! One person starts the song and then the next person begins at the next line, so you're all singing together but different parts.'

'Like "London's Burning",' Aziza said, remembering the song she'd learnt at school.

'That doesn't sound like a very happy song,' Peri said.

Aziza giggled. 'You're right – it's about a big fire. I think I'd much prefer to learn Sirena's song!'

They swam in a line as Sirena taught them the song. Even her pet seahorse, Water Dancer, joined in.

'*Ocean dreaming, ocean feeling,*

Water flowing, water showing,

High tide, waves we ride,

With Mami Wata, problems shatter.'

Soon they were all singing together, one after each other. Aziza had never thought she could sing very well, but actually, it sounded pretty good when they were all singing together. Maybe it was like everything else – working in a team made things easier!

They kept on singing even as they swam into a thick kelp forest. Again, Aziza was very thankful for Tiko's lamp. She stuck close by him, weaving between the thick fronds that seemed to rise higher than a block of flats. There were different types of creatures down here – Sirena introduced them to flat rays and orange rockfish, and even a friendly sea turtle.

They were about to emerge from the kelp forest when she heard a yelp from behind her. She spun around and saw Sirena struggling beside a towering kelp tree. Her long locs were somehow tangled around the branches. Water Dancer was panicking, darting around Sirena's head while she thrashed about, trying to untangle herself.

'Sirena!' Peri said, rushing over and trying to help. 'You're really stuck!'

'I know,' Sirena wailed. 'Be careful! Kelp trees can release poison if they're disturbed too much.'

Aziza flicked her tail to move forward and reached out to put her hands on Sirena's shoulders. 'Don't worry!

I'm great at detangling hair. You just need a little bit of patience. Can I try?'

Sirena nodded just slightly. 'Oh yes, please. Thank you!'

Aziza worked quickly, her fingers carefully unravelling Sirena's locs from the branches of the kelp tree. Without thinking, she began humming the song they'd been singing earlier, and soon everyone joined in. It seemed to calm Sirena, who stopped moving her head and trying to touch her hair, letting Aziza get to work.

'There you go!' said Aziza as she released

Sirena's very last loc from the kelp tree.

Sirena flung her arms around her. 'Thank you! I thought I was about to get a very horrible rash! I'm really sorry for slowing us down.'

'It wasn't your fault,' Aziza said, smiling. She found a long ribbon of seaweed and tied Sirena's hair up in a high ponytail.

Sirena looked at

herself in a bit of sea glass. 'I love it. Thank you.'

The friends were on the move again and now the ocean was indigo-blue. Without Tiko's lamp, they wouldn't have been able to see more than a couple of metres in front of them.

'That's it!' Sirena pointed straight ahead, to a patch of totally black ocean. Opal Trench.

It was filled with some of the strangest creatures Aziza had ever seen. There were little fish with gaping mouths and sharp teeth, and see-through glowing jellyfish that looked like they had wires of electricity threaded through them. There was even a tiny fish with ball-like eyes that flashed in and out of sight.

'That's a hatchetfish,' Sirena explained. 'It can make itself invisible!'

Tiko's nose twitched and his eyes flicked about. 'How cool would it be to shape-shift into one of these?'

'Nooo!' everyone screamed in unison.

'Please don't change, Tiko. We need you for your light!' Peri explained.

Tiko chuckled. 'Ha, I knew it was the right decision to be an anglerfish!'

'I never doubted it for a second,' Peri winked.

'So if this is Opal Trench, where could the conch shell be?' Aziza wondered out loud.

'Maybe the creatures here have seen it?'

Peri said. 'Hello, excuse me?' she started to say to a hatchetfish, but it darted away so quickly Peri didn't get to finish her question.

Tiko swam towards one of the electric jellyfish, but it buzzed brightly as if in warning and he flung himself backwards with a yelp. 'Furballs! They're not so friendly down here, are they?'

'Don't be offended,' came a soft, low voice behind them. 'We don't get many visitors here in the Opal Trench. The jellyfish aren't used to strangers.'

Aziza turned around and came face to face

with a small yellow octopus with little flappy ears, like an elephant. It might have been the cutest thing she'd ever seen in the ocean! She waved.

The octopus smiled. 'But me? I like to chat,' the creature went on. 'Will you stick around and keep me company?'

Aziza shook her head regretfully. 'It's really nice to meet you but we're on an urgent quest. Maybe you can help us?'

'I'm all ears.' The octopus said this with a little chuckle that made Aziza smile as well.

'We're looking for a special conch shell.' Sirena sounded a little impatient, but Aziza knew by now that Sirena didn't mean to be rude – she was just determined to find the conch shell. 'We think it's buried somewhere here.'

'Buried? That I can help you with!'

Without taking a breath, the cute octopus opened her mouth wide and began tunnelling away at the seabed with her jaws. Sand flew everywhere.

'Wow!' Tiko said. 'I was not expecting that! I know what I'll be shifting into next!'

The friends jumped back to avoid the sand shower. They couldn't really see what the octopus was doing – she was moving superfast and her digging was creating a tremendous sand storm. But just moments later, everything stopped. The falling sand settled like snowflakes in a snow globe.

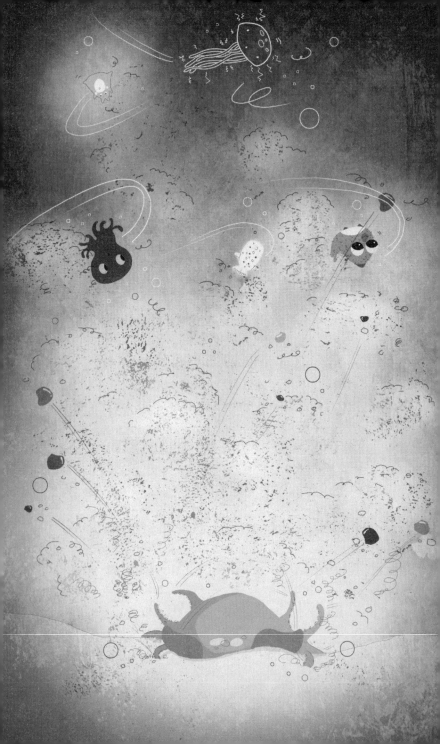

The next moment, the octopus appeared, clutching a sparkling white conch shell in her tentacles!

Chapter 7

'Is this what you're looking for?' the octopus

asked, holding out the conch shell and

grinning. At least Aziza *thought* it was a

grin – it was hard

to tell when

her mouth was edged by tentacles.

'Oh yes!' squealed Peri. 'Thank you.
THANK YOU!'

The octopus stopped smiling. 'I guess that
means you'll be leaving me now.'

Aziza felt terrible when she saw how sad
the octopus looked.

'It does. I'm sorry,' said Sirena. 'But . . .' She
beckoned to Water Dancer and whispered in
her ear. 'My pet seahorse will stay with you
for a while to have a play date. How does
that sound?'

Now the octopus spun on the spot. 'Just

perfect! You're so kind.' She handed the shiny conch shell to Peri. The princess kissed the shell before tucking it under her arm.

'Now let's get back to Shimmerton!' she cried.

They waved to the octopus and Water Dancer as the pair settled down in the sand to talk.

The four friends were soon shooting through the dark water, racing back to Shimmerton beach as fast as they could. Their tails flapped so hard they were almost blurs.

I hope I get to swim in the sea on our camping holiday, Aziza thought. *But I'll need a wet suit and I'll really miss my mermaid's tail . . .* She decided she wouldn't even mind if it was raining on holiday – it wouldn't matter about being wet if she was in the water anyway!

They made it through the kelp forest without getting stuck this time, thanks to Sirena's hair being safely tied back. Soon the water around them became brighter and Aziza guessed they were nearing the beach. She realized she hadn't run out of energy at ALL, even though they'd been swimming for AGES.

'Hey, Sirena,' Aziza said. 'Why aren't I tired after swimming for so long?'

Sirena flicked her tail to turn to Aziza. 'Mermaid magic, of course!' she drawled. 'Mermaids never get tired of swimming. That goes for mermaid fairies too!'

Aziza felt her skin prickle with goosebumps at the magic of it all. But she couldn't forget the humongous problem in Shimmerton, mermaid magic or not. What would the shell-walker be doing when they got back?

They arrived on the shore of the beach and Sirena lifted her hand and traced a new symbol on the water. The sea glittered all around them and Aziza's body tingled as she watched her tail shimmer back into her legs once more. The playsuit she was wearing wasn't even wet – nor was her hair – thanks

to mermaid magic! Peri had lost her tail as well.

Tiko's nose began to twitch and he sneezed, super loudly. He disappeared behind a cloud of sparkles, and when they faded away, he was no longer an anglerfish, but back to his normal cuddly self.

'Thank you, Sirena, I—' Aziza broke off. Sirena sat in the shallows with her mouth downturned, staring longingly at the beach.

'Are you OK?' Aziza asked her.

Sirena shrugged. 'I guess. I . . . just wish I could come on shore, like Cante can.' She lifted an arm to point to the Encantado who was sprinting across the sand. He was now in human form, but Aziza recognized the dolphin-like nose.

Aziza watched as Cante chased the shell-walker back and forth across the sand. He was joined by Mr Bracken and Alf, the Elf and Safety Officer, and Mrs Sayeed. *Guess they never managed to get the shell-walker back into its hole . . . but at least it was still on the beach*, Aziza thought. The creature was bigger than ever, its shell-like scales hidden by all the items that had stuck to it – deckchairs, picnic blankets, beach balls. There was even a beach flag sticking up from its back.

'Keep away from it!' Alf was calling, his cheeks puffed out. 'Everyone must stay back! Or you'll end up stuck to its side as well!'

Peri held up the conch shell. 'We've got something to help!' she cried. 'This will solve all our problems.'

Cante ran over. 'Quick, what are you waiting for?' he said breathlessly. 'Come over and use it. We need to get the shell-walker under control!'

Aziza looked back at Sirena, feeling sad they were leaving her behind.

'Go,' Sirena murmured. 'I'll stay here. Mermaids belong in the water. That's just the way it is.'

'That's what they said about dolphins once

but my ancestors soon changed that,' Cante said. 'I can lend you some of my powers to come on land – if you want?'

'Really?' Sirena said. 'That'd be AMAZING!'

The Encantado stepped close to Sirena and began running around her in a circle, kicking up water everywhere.

'Look, my tail is gone,' Sirena said, jumping up. 'Whoa, this feels weird.' She swayed for a moment.

Aziza took her arm. 'Don't worry, I've got you.'

Everyone ran across the beach. Peri was holding the shimmering white conch shell aloft.

With everything stuck to it, the shell-walker was now as big as an oak tree. Alf was frantically waving his hands, trying to keep it distracted so it wouldn't escape from the beach and into Shimmerton.

'Quick, blow into the shell!' Sirena told Peri.

Peri nodded and put the shell to her lips. Everyone stopped as a high whistling note came from the shell.

Everyone except the shell-walker.

'It's not working!' Peri wailed. 'I thought the conch would put the shell-walker to sleep or something?' Peri tried to blow harder. 'Am I doing it wrong?' She passed the conch shell to Tiko, but the exact same note sounded out when he tried, and the shell-walker didn't take any notice.

Tiko passed the shell to Aziza. 'Furballs! You try!' He started to pace backwards and forwards.

Aziza tried blowing gently at first, then blew really hard. The same sound that had sounded for the others came out now and the shell-walker was most definitely NOT

falling asleep. '*Glittersticks!*'

Alf, Mr Bracken, Mrs Sayeed and Cante were jumping up and down now in front of the creature, right at the edge of the beach. The shell-walker would escape onto the path to town any moment if they didn't think of something, fast.

Chapter 8

Aziza tried to tune out the sound of her friends panicking and the shell-walker stomping around as she thought about the problem – and all the other problems – they'd solved on their quest to find the conch shell. *We all*

believed the shell's song would put the shell-walker

to sleep! But . . . why did we think that? The

legend never said that. It just said the conch shell

would solve our problem.

She thought of how Sirena's song earlier made her feel relaxed and less stressed, just like a lullaby. 'Maybe our problem is that we are expecting the shell to do all the work for us,' she whispered. 'What if we actually have to find the answer ourselves? Just like we solved the riddle!'

'Sirena!' Aziza called out. Her friends spun round to look at her. 'Can we try singing your song again? It made me so relaxed and calm when you were singing it – maybe that will work better than the conch shell and put the shell-walker to sleep?'

The mermaid looked confused at first, but then nodded. 'Trying is the important thing, right?' She began to sing the song she'd taught them all earlier . . .

But Aziza quickly realized that was no good – no one could hear it over the commotion on the beach.

'We need to sing it together, like before!' Aziza said, and started to join in.

Tiko stopped pacing and began singing too, and Peri soon followed. Now the song was louder – but could the shell-walker hear it?

Something strange and amazingly magical happened then. The other residents of Shimmerton on the beach began to join in too. The song grew louder and louder:

'*Ocean dreaming, ocean feeling,*

Water flowing, water showing,

High tide, waves we ride,

With Mami Wata, problems shatter.'

Aziza looked around and even saw the Gigglers singing, mouths wide, as they hid – not very well – behind a palm tree. She remembered Felly's voice being . . . um . . . not the greatest, but singing with others seemed to help her too.

The beach-goers had turned into the most amazing choir, their song echoing across the beach. Even Officer Alf, Mr Bracken, Mrs Sayeed and Cante had joined in. No longer trying to distract the shell-walker but just standing very still.

Aziza wasn't sure if she was imagining it,

but something seemed to be happening to the creature. The shell-walker wasn't rushing forwards any more and its movements were becoming slower and slower. As Aziza looked on and the choir went on singing, the shell-walker began drifting from side to side, as if in a daze.

'Oh wow!' breathed Peri, as one by one things started to fall off the creature: first a parasol, then a picnic bench and a surfboard.

'Keep singing!' Aziza whispered to her friend. This was working, but they couldn't stop yet. The crowd continued singing while

they watched the shell-walker shrink in front of their eyes. Items were falling off it like leaves from autumn trees as it plodded back oh-so-slowly towards the huge hole it had emerged from.

'*Ocean dreaming, ocean feeling,*' sang Aziza,

staring at the shell-walker. It was back to its normal tiny size and nearly at the hole. Just as she sang '*Water flowing, water showing,*' the shell-walker reached the edge of the hole, took one more step forward and then . . . toppled in!

Peri flew towards the hole, still singing. Aziza joined her in the sky, wriggling her shoulders to fly just like Peri had taught her to on her first visit to Shimmerton. They looked down and saw the shell-walker curled up in a ball, fast asleep.

'Phew!' Peri whispered, careful not to wake up the creature.

Tiko and Sirena were running across the beach below, followed by the rest of the crowd.

Officer Alf waved his hands to get everyone's attention. 'We must fill in the hole as quickly as we can,' he whisper-shouted. 'So that the creature can stay nice and warm and stay asleep!'

Everyone began shovelling sand into the hole, some using buckets and spades that had fallen off the shell-walker on its way to the hole. It seemed like everyone Aziza knew was there – even Zorigami, the clockmaker.

She blinked when she spotted Noon's bright-pink hair over the other side of the hole. The rest of the Gigglers were there too, all looking extremely sheepish.

'We're really sorry,' said Noon.

Felly looked up with wide eyes. 'We promise not to dig a hole that deep ever again! Right, Kendra?'

Aziza thought she saw Kendra pulling a face, but it WAS hard to tell from the other side of the large hole. 'Yes,' Kendra said eventually. 'We're sorry!'

Peri turned to Aziza with a shocked look on her face. 'Did the Gigglers just say sorry?' she whispered.

With everyone helping, the hole was soon completely filled. Aziza sighed – she was happy they'd stopped the shell-walker from destroying everything, but she knew that it meant something else, too. It was time for her to go home.

'I should get going,' Aziza said to her friends as they walked away from the hole.

'Oh no, you can't go yet!' Sirena cried. 'We've only just started to get to know each other!'

Peri put an arm around Sirena. 'Don't worry, Aziza always comes back. We'll have other adventures together, for sure!'

'Hmm, OK.' Sirena smiled. 'But I'll miss you.'

'I'll miss you too,' Aziza replied, and she realized she really meant it. She thought of Sirena as a friend now. Aziza hadn't needed to worry about her place in the group being taken. There was room for them all!

Peri, Sirena and Tiko walked Aziza back to the fairy door, hidden in the trunk of the palm tree. It started to shimmer as they drew nearer.

Aziza turned to her friends. 'See you soon!'

They wrapped each other into a group hug.

'You have a sunny time back home,

won't you Aziza?' Sirena said.

Aziza gave one last squeeze in the hug before stepping away. 'I'll do my best.' She turned the jewelled doorknob and walked through. As golden light flashed around her like sunlight, Aziza remembered Sirena's words. She was pretty sure she wasn't going to have a sunny time camping, but that didn't matter. Whatever problem the weather threw at her family she knew they'd work it out!

The next moment, Aziza was standing in her bedroom, her half-filled rucksack on the bed in front of her. When she turned around and looked through the window, she gasped. Sunlight was streaming into the room, and when she looked outside, there wasn't a single cloud in the bright-blue sky.

She knew she hadn't been gone for long.

Time moved much quicker in Shimmerton than at home. But how had the weather changed so quickly? It had been grey and pouring with rain when she left. *Could it be . . . mermaid magic?* she wondered, thinking back to Sirena's last words to her. *Have a sunny time.* She closed her eyes and let the sunshine warm her face. *Now Mum will be happy*, Aziza thought. They'd all go on sunny hikes together and swim in the sea. Maybe they'd even sing camp songs around a fire before bedtime. And Aziza knew exactly which song she'd sing.

Myths and Legends

Aziza, her friends and the inhabitants of Shimmerton are inspired by myths and legends from all around the world:

Aziza is named after a type of fairy creature. In West African folklore, specifically *Dahomey mythology*, the Aziza are helpful fairies who live in the forest and are full of wisdom.

Peri's name comes from ancient Persian mythology. Peris are winged spirits who can be kind and helpful, but they also sometimes enjoy playing tricks on people. In paintings they are usually shown with large, bird-like wings.

In Philippine mythology, *Sirena* is the name for a mermaid with a beautiful singing voice. Her sea-creature friends are normally close by.

The **shell-walker** is a creature from Icelandic folklore. Shell-walkers have humped backs and are covered in a coat of thick, rattling shells. They have lots of names, but in Icelandic they are called *Skeljalalli*.

Mami Water is a **goddess** and **deity**. She is often depicted as a beautiful mermaid and protector of women and children. The tales told about her span from West Africa all the way to the Caribbean and South America.

Mrs Sayeed is an **Almiraj**, a legendary rabbit with a unicorn-like horn. They're found in Arabic myths and folklore.

Phoenixes, like Mr Phoenix, are mystical, bird-like creatures found in Greek mythology. They are said to be immortal and have healing powers. The phoenix is one of the most well-known myths.

Neith is the ancient Egyptian goddess of war and weaving. The ancient Egyptians believed she was wise, powerful and helped settle disputes between other gods.

Unicorns, like Mr Bracken, Fern and Finn, have appeared in folklore for thousands of years. They're normally portrayed as magical, horned white horses and are said to have healing powers.

Gnomes are small, mythical creatures that appear in myths and fairy tales from all over Europe. They are said to live in meadows, woodlands and underground.

The **cyclops** is a one-eyed giant that appears in Greek and Roman mythology. Cyclopes were skilled builders and blacksmiths.

Pixies are mythological creatures from English folktales. They are tiny, magical creatures – a bit like fairies – but they don't have wings.

Cante is an Amazon river dolphin called an **Encantado**. According to South American legends, they come from an underwater realm called Encanto and are able to shape-shift into humans.

The **Makara** is a sea creature found in Hindu mythology. It can take the form of many different animals, but is always the guardian of gateways and protector of important entryways.

The **Zorigami** is based on a Japanese myth about a clock that comes to life after one hundred years.

Join Aziza on her brand new
magical adventure in

Aziza's Secret Fairy Door and the Magic Puppy

Coming in February 2023

Chapter 1

'But my friend Jola has a dog?' Otis put down his fork and crossed his arms.

Aziza saw her dad share a look with Mum across the dinner table. Dad then sighed deeply. 'We've been through this, Otis.'

'The flat is too small,' Mum added with a sympathetic smile. 'You wouldn't want the dog to feel all cooped up, would you? Dogs need lots of space.'

Aziza pushed at a piece of fried plantain on her plate. She'd lost count of the number of times her brother had begged their parents for a pet. But the answer was always the same.

'I could make room. And we have the balcony,' Otis pleaded. 'I'd take it out for a walk every day so it wouldn't feel all cooped up.'

'I'd help too,' Aziza offered.

'I'm sorry, kids. We're also not allowed big pets in the flat,' Dad said. 'How about a goldfish instead? They're cute.'

'A goldfish?' Otis exclaimed with a horrified expression. 'They're not cute. They're boring. You can't teach them tricks or take them for a walk.'

Aziza secretly agreed, but she knew better than to get involved with this argument. *It's not like it's Mum and Dad's fault we can't get a dog.*

Otis pushed his plate of half-finished food away. 'It's just not fair!' he muttered under his breath.

Aziza's dad shared another look with Mum but she just shook her head with a sad-looking smile.

The rest of dinner went quietly. When they were finished, Mum asked Aziza and Otis to clear the table.

'You know what, Otis,' Aziza said as she stacked the plates, 'maybe a goldfish wouldn't be so bad?'

Otis's face creased into an annoyed frown. 'You're right. Having a goldfish wouldn't be bad – it would be terrible. I want a dog.'

'I was just . . .'

'Just leave it,' Otis interrupted. 'You wouldn't understand. All you care about are those pretend fairies.'

Aziza gasped. 'That's not very nice.'

Otis looked down but still wore a stubborn expression on his face.

'Fine,' Aziza said, putting the plate in her hand down. 'You can finish cleaning up by yourself then.'

Aziza walked away. Out of the corner of her eye she thought she saw her brother looking a bit guilty, but she couldn't be sure.

★

Aziza shut her bedroom door with a soft click. *It's not my fault Otis can't have a pet*, she thought. *Why is he taking it out on me?*

Tick, tock, tick, tock.

Aziza paused. She didn't have a ticking clock in her room. She turned towards the sound. It was coming from the fairy door that sat on her windowsill. The door was covered in tiny spring blossoms and green leaves.

She rushed over to it, forgetting all about Otis and their argument. The tick, tocking got louder and the doorknob was glowing. Aziza reached for it and felt a shiver of anticipation race through her body. *I'm going back to the magical world of Shimmerton!* She thought. *I'll get to see Peri and Tiko again!* The fairy door opened, bathing Aziza in a golden beam of light. However, just as she stepped through, her bedroom door crashed open with a loud bang. Aziza whipped around.

'I'm sorry, Zizi,' Otis began. 'I didn't mean to—whoa!' he exclaimed. 'What's going on here?'

Otis's dark-brown eyes were super wide.

Uh-oh, Aziza thought. She was the only one in her world who knew about the magic of the fairy door. *Not any more*, Aziza realized.

Aziza opened her mouth to explain, but she could feel herself shrinking as she got pulled through the door.

'Wait! Where are you going?' Otis raced towards her. Aziza saw the fairy door's golden beam cover him too, and then he was pulled through the doorway with her.

Soon they were through to the other side. Aziza and Otis stared at each other as they found themselves on a cobbled path, surrounded by rolling green hills.

'That whole door thing was awesome,' Otis

said, 'but I have some questions.'

'So do I,' Aziza responded. 'Why did you follow me?'

'You're my sister, Aziza,' Otis explained patiently. 'What kind of big brother would let you go through some strange magical door by yourself? Now we just need to figure out what's going on.'

Aziza raised an eyebrow. 'Maybe I know what's going on.'

Otis looked surprised and then grinned. 'You do? Spill the beans.' He looked around. Aziza saw his mouth drop open as he took in the pink sky, swirled with candy-floss-coloured clouds, and the jewel-toned shops that lined Shimmerton's high street in the distance. 'They eat beans here, right?' Otis added.

Aziza smiled, remembering how amazing it had felt the first time she came through the fairy door. 'They eat beans and lots of other cools things as well,' she reassured him.

'Where are we?' Otis looked back at the closed fairy door. Its edges were already blending into the side of the flagstone wall. 'The door's disappeared!'

'It does that,' Aziza replied. Her dungarees had been replaced by a pretty dress with pockets. It was covered in tiny flowers that complemented the butterfly wings that now sprouted from her back. 'We're in the magical kingdom of Shimmerton,' Aziza added.

'It's incredible,' Otis breathed in awe. 'How many times have you been here?'

'Quite a few,' Aziza admitted. 'The first time I came through was the day I got the fairy door.'

'No wonder you've been so into fairies,' Otis said. 'I mean, more than usual. You've been hiding this the whole time.' Otis turned around, trying to get a better look at their surroundings.

'Hey, you've got wings too!' Aziza gasped, spying a silvery set of dragonfly wings at his back.

'YES,' Otis exclaimed, spinning on the spot and trying to get a better look. 'Oooh, I'm going to fly!' He wriggled his shoulders and leapt into the air. But he dropped straight back down again.

'They don't work!' Otis grumbled. 'What's wrong with them?'

'It takes a lot of practice,' Aziza explained as she fluttered her own. 'It took Peri ages to teach me.'

'Who's Peri?'

Aziza smiled. She was actually really loving that her brother was here. 'She's my friend. She's also the princess of Shimmerton, but she's not a big fan of princess dresses or doing the other boring things that come with the job. Then there's Tiko, he's a shape-shifter. He's super sweet and brave.'

Otis stared at Aziza in amazement. 'A shape-shifter?'

'You'll see,' Aziza grabbed her brother's arm. 'There are so many magical creatures that live here. I can't wait for you to meet them all.'

'It doesn't seem like *anybody* lives here,' Otis said with a doubtful look around.

Aziza followed his gaze. Otis was right. There was no one on the path or on the high street. *Glittersticks! Where is everybody?* Aziza thought.

'Wait a sec,' Otis said, pointing to a small sign just up ahead. 'I think that's our answer.'

Aziza went over to get a closer look,

Otis followed close behind her.

THIS WAY TO THE SPRING FETE

The letters were written in gold paint and beneath them was a big arrow pointing towards the high street.

'Of course!' Aziza said, clapping her hands. 'They must all be at the fete. Let's go and find Peri and Tiko.'

About the Authors

Lola Morayo is the pen name for the creative partnership of writers Tọ́lá Okogwu and Jasmine Richards.

Tọ́lá is a journalist and author of the Daddy Do My Hair series. She is an avid reader who enjoys spending time with her family and friends in her home in Kent, where she lives with her husband and daughters.

© Karen Ball

Jasmine is the founder of an inclusive fiction studio called Storymix and has written more than fifteen books for children. She lives in Hertfordshire with her husband and two children.

Both are passionate about telling stories that are inclusive and joyful.

About the Illustrator

© Katarina Tibenska

Cory Reid lives in Kettering and is an illustrator and designer who has worked in the creative industry for more than fifteen years, with clients including Usborne Publishing, Owlet Press and Card Factory.